MW00916678

This book is dedicated to anyone who needs a friend.

- Nahla Skye


This book is dedicated to my 4th/5th grade teacher, Mrs. Susan Grice.

- Vernisha Crawford

# NAHLA AND AMY-G
## Visit Amygdala World

Nahla Skye and Vernisha Crawford

Hi, my name is Nahla.
I have three best friends.
This is my Mom. She is my best friend #1.
My mom is a business owner.

This is my Dad. He is my best friend #2.
He works in tall buildings and wears nice clothes.

I love my family, but we are not perfect.
My Mom and my Dad do not live together.

Sometimes I stay with my Mom.
Sometimes I stay with my Dad.
I know they love me very much.
But sometimes, it can feel hard.

That's where my best friend #3 comes in.
Her name is Amy-G!
Amy-G is a bird from Amygdala World.
Did you know it's a real place inside your brain?
It's true!

When you need to do something brave,
Amy-G comes out.
You can feel her in your body.
But that's not all.
Come on. I'll show you.

To get to Amygdala World...
Clap your hands together one time.
Now rub them together really fast for 10 seconds.
Let's count down from 10.

10·9·8

10 - 9 - 8 - 7 - 6 - 5 - 4 - 3 - 2 -1
Now take a deep breath
and let Amy-G appear.

"Hi, Amy-G! How are you feeling?" asks Nahla.

"Hi, Nahla! I'm feeling warm, tingly, and excited to see you!" replies Amy-G.

"Nice! Will you show me and my new friends around Amygdala world?" asks Nahla.

"Of course, Nahla!" says Amy-G.
"But first, there are two things you need to know.

#1 - I am the protector of Amygdala World.
My job is to keep you safe.

#2 - Everybody has an Amygdala World in their
brains but it looks and feels different.

Now let's go see yours!"

Our first stop is Nahla's Home," says Amy-G.

IT'S A CASTLE!" yells Nahla with excitement.

"That's right—a castle. It's a place that makes YOU feel safe," says Amy-G

"Inside are all your favo... Unicorns, rainbows, books, and...

"My favorite animal is a Panda!" s...

"It is! There is also a waterfall that changes colors," says Amy-G.

e my home. It makes me feel so good inside!" says Nahla. "The waterfall is my favorite. But why does it change colors?" asks Nahla.

"Great question Nahla. It changes colors when your feelings and emotions change."

When you're feeling happy, the waterfall turns pink.

When you're feeling confused, it turns gray.

When you're feeling angry, it turns red.

When you're feeling relaxed, it turns green.

When you're feeling afraid, it turns yellow.

When you're feeling sad, it turns blue.

When you're feeling confident, it turns orange.

When you're feeling grateful, it turns purple.

"Wow! Does everyone have a waterfall in their Amygdala World?" asks Nahla.

"Yes," says Amy-G. "And they have a bird like me! I was born the same day you were. That's why I'm your best friend! You have more friends too!

When you have a positive connection another bird like me arrives," says Amy-G

"That's really cool! But Amy-G? What is a connection?" asks Nahla.

"A connection is a link between you and a person, place, or thing. Like your family, friends, school, and dance class. The more positive connections you have, the more birds you have," replies Amy-G.

"Oh yes! I love to DANCE! What happens when I don't have a positive connection?" asks Nahla.

"Another great question, Nahla.
I'll explain at our next stop; Brick Land.
Let's follow the river from the waterfall, into the
woods, and cross the swinging bridge."

Nahla and Amy-G continue to walk and talk. When they get to the swinging bridge, Nahla stops.

"Amy-G, I don't want to cross the swinging bridge. It's scary."

"Yes. I can see that you are feeling afraid. I noticed the waterfall turn yellow. Let's get some help and support. Just say this chant with me," says Amy-G.

"Support. Support. I need support!"
"Support. Support. I need support!"

Nahla and Amy-G yell the chant together.
Hundreds of birds appear in the sky.

"Wow! There are so many!" says Nahla.

"Yes, it is. Now tell them how you feel."

"Hi Birdies, I feel scared," mumbles Nahla.

"Now tell them what you need," says Amy-G.

"I need help crossing the bridge."

The birds gather around Nahla, lifting her off the ground to fly over the swinging bridge.

Once they land in Brick Land, Nahla shivers.

"It's very cold and empty here. This doesn't feel like a happy place."

"It's not," replies Amy-G. "When you have a connection that is not a positive one, a brick appears here in brick land."

"I don't like this place, Amy-G," says Nahla.

"I understand," replies Amy-G.
"We don't like to visit Brick Land but it is a part of you. When things get tough in the real world, sometimes we get stuck here."

"I do not want to be stuck in Brick Land. Can we go back home now?" asks Nahla.

"Of course!" says Amy-G. "Moving our bodies helps us get away from Brick Land. Come on, do the safety dance with me."

Hands up! Hands Down! Let's turn around.
Shake it to the left. Shake it to the right.
Wiggle down to safety to be ALRIGHT!

Nahla and Amy-G do the safety dance over and over. The waterfall turns pink. Before you know it, Nahla is back home, safe, with her family.

Where will Nahla and Amy-G visit next?

We will see next time...

THE END.

Made in the USA
Columbia, SC
22 May 2024

36082568R00020